Wings
of
Terror

Dragon Riders of Osnen Book 5

RICHARD FIERCE

Dragonfire Press

Copyright © 2020 Richard Fierce

Cover design by germancreative.

Cover art by Rosauro Ugang

ISBN: 978-1-947329-35-5

CONTENTS

1

"He's been here."

I looked up at Maren as she returned to our makeshift camp. The locals in the village were skittish around Sion, so I'd decided it was better to keep our distance. A small stream flowed nearby and provided a peaceful atmosphere, which was a radical change from the last few days.

"Another body?" I asked.

Maren offered a stiff nod and sat across from me at the cooking fire. I'd caught a few fish from the stream and they were nearly done. Sion was curled up in front of a large tree, her eyes watching us.

"Are you sure it was Demris? Ever since we lost his trail, we haven't found any signs of his presence."

"It was him," Maren replied. "One of the villagers is a sorceress and cast a warding spell that forced him to flee. She described the green smoke."

Maren was right. That was definitely him. The nightmarish image of the green smoke coming out of the ferryman's mouth had been burned into my mind's eye with glaring detail. I nodded but didn't say anything. We sat quietly, but there was no silence. The fish meat sizzled and the stream babbled.

I grabbed onto the stick I'd impaled the fish on and lifted it off the fire and set it aside to let the meat cool. Once they weren't too hot to eat, Maren and I ate our fill. I laid on the ground and propped my head upon a smooth rock I'd pulled from the stream.

"How long ago did he come through here?" I asked.

"A day and a half," Maren replied. "The sorceress was shaken up. She said she put all of her strength into that spell and it almost wasn't enough."

"Did she know she was up against the soul of a dragon?"

"No, I don't think so. I just don't understand, Eldwin. He wouldn't kill people without a reason."

"Unless he's gone rogue," I said. "Maybe coming back from the island did something to him and he's turned evil."

"No," Maren replied. She was adamant in her opinion that there was another reason for Demris's actions, but I wasn't so sure.

"If we don't find him soon, we're going to have other problems," I said.

"What do you mean?"

"We're far enough away that the Citadel probably won't hear about this, but Katori is likely to hear about it if she hasn't already. And considering she knows where we were going, she'll probably come looking for answers. And for us."

"So? We'll tell her the truth," Maren replied.

"We don't know the truth. At least, not about Demris's actions."

"I know he's not evil," she said defensively.

"Maren, I get it. You were bonded to Demris, so you have a biased view of him. But you can't stay blind. You need to realize that something has happened that made him change."

"Stop it!" Maren shouted. "Just stop it, Eldwin! You don't know that!"

Maren rose to her feet and stormed off into the woods. I sighed and looked at Sion.

What do you think? I asked her.

You make a valid argument, but Maren is still grieving. She needs more time before she will be open to what you say.

I know, I replied. *Yet the longer it takes her to realize the truth, the more people will die because of Demris.*

Maren knows this. It puts a burden on her, I'm sure.

I ground my teeth in frustration, but what else could I do? I couldn't force Maren into seeing that something was wrong with Demris.

"She'll see it when she's ready," I whispered.

Eventually, Maren returned to the camp. She remained aloof and didn't make eye contact with me. I could tell she was still upset, so I didn't try talking to her. Instead, we started breaking down our camp. I put the fire out and filled my canteen with water from the stream, then Maren and I mounted Sion.

"Head southwest," Maren said. "The sorceress said Demris went in that direction."

If you would, I told Sion.

She launched into the air, the wind from her powerful wings blowing the treetops around wildly. Sion ascended higher and higher, then leveled out and flew in the direction Maren had said. I considered the situation and there was one thing I couldn't figure out. Whether Demris had turned evil or not, it didn't make sense that he was staying in the area. He was moving from place to place, but he wasn't heading toward the Citadel. If anything, he was traveling in a giant circle.

You wonder if he's searching for something? Sion asked.

Yes, but what?

I'm not sure. He should be heading for his body.

That's what I've been thinking. So why isn't he? I asked.

Sion snorted in reply and continued flying. I turned my attention to the ground below and looked for signs of towns or villages. The time slid by and I traced my finger along the edges of Sion's scales in boredom.

"Smoke ahead!" Maren shouted. She leaned against me and pointed to the right.

I spotted the smoke, too. It wasn't green, but it was more than I would expect to see coming from a small settlement.

Take us down, I told Sion.

She banked right and descended. As we got lower, I could see a building was on fire and people were running.

"Demris might be here!" I shouted over my shoulder. "Get ready!"

Sion swooped down and landed outside the village. Maren leaped to the ground and sprinted to the building. I followed after her and glanced around, looking for green smoke. A man carrying a bucket full of water almost ran into me.

"Apologies!" The man called out as he continued past. I jogged to catch up with him.

"What happened?" I asked.

"Thomas set his own place on fire after something possessed his wife. We're trying to put out the fire to keep it from spreading."

I slowed my pace. The man reached the building and flung the water at the flames that spouted out of a window. Maren was nearby and lifted her hand. I could see her lips moving and guessed she was casting a spell. A moment later, my guess was confirmed as the flames died abruptly.

A woman staggered out of the structure and fell

to her knees. Her flesh was badly burned and smoke wafted off her. Maren stepped closer to her, but she jumped back when the woman's head shot back and her mouth opened in a silent scream. Green smoke poured out of her mouth.

"Do something!" I shouted at Maren.

She looked at me, then back at the smoke. Maren closed her eyes and began chanting. The smoke expanded and grew, taking a draconic shape. The details of the dragon's face were skeletal and looked more like the dracolich we'd defeated than I cared to think about.

There was a bright flash of light from Maren's hand, and Demris roared and tried to flee, but he was held in place. Maren's face contorted with her concentration and she seemed to be struggling to keep Demris ensorcelled. There was nothing I could do to help except to keep the villagers away. The man who'd been carrying the bucket kept his distance and helped me keep the others from coming closer.

The woman Demris had possessed was lying on the ground. I wanted to help her, but I didn't think it was wise to get that close until Maren had Demris under control. Maren cried out in anguish and the spell was broken. The strength of Demris's color intensified and the surrounding buildings burst into flame, then he fled, shooting through the sky faster than anything I'd seen before.

"No!" Maren screamed.

The men and women I'd kept at bay rushed into

the area, dousing the flames with buckets of water. I rushed to Maren and embraced her. Her body shook with her sobs.

"I'm sorry," she whispered. "I tried to keep him from leaving, but he was too strong."

"It's all right," I said. "We'll find him again."

The villagers finished putting out the fires and dealt with the woman Demris had possessed, who was now dead. I released Maren and put my arm around her shoulder and led her out of the village. Sion was waiting for us.

I saw him escape, she said.

Unfortunately, Maren's spell couldn't keep him in place.

Are we going after him?

Did you see which way he went? I asked.

West.

I wish we knew what he was after. It would make it a little easier to track him.

The will of the dead is unknown, Sion replied.

I helped Maren up Sion's shoulder and looked back at the village. The people were terrified, justifiably so, but until we could come back here and tell them that everything was safe again, I knew they would live in constant fear of Demris's return. I joined Maren on Sion's back and watched the village grow smaller as Sion ascended into the sky.

I knew Maren would probably hate me for it, but

I decided that if we couldn't stop Demris soon, I was going to fly to the Citadel and alert Anesko.

2

I awoke suddenly.

The stars shone above me and I listened intently to my surroundings, trying to determine what roused me. A gentle wind was blowing, but otherwise, there was nothing out of the ordinary. I rolled onto my side and saw Maren was still asleep beside me. Her chest rose and fell rhythmically with her breathing. It was the most peaceful I'd seen her in days.

Sion was also asleep, but she stirred fitfully and growled. The bond flooded with her anxiety, but I quickly erected a mental barrier to keep it at bay. I got up, careful not to wake Maren, and walked over to Sion and rested a hand gently on her head. Her growling stopped, but she continued to twitch. I assumed she was having another nightmare about her days of being tortured by Rory and his wizard.

A clattering noise startled me, and I looked in the direction the sound had come from. We were in a heavily wooded area and it was difficult to see anything other than shadows. I retrieved my sword from where I'd been sleeping and unsheathed it, then headed toward the sound. It was likely a wild animal, but I wanted to be sure we had nothing to worry about.

I walked as quietly as I could, trying not to step too heavily. The clattering sound filled the air again and I paused. I could hear a voice muttering, but I wasn't able to make out the words. I brought my sword up and peered around the thick trunk of a tree.

A shaft of moonlight poured through the canopy overhead, revealing a short figure stacking rocks in a pile. They were wearing a hooded robe and had their back to me. I glanced back to where Maren and Sion were. The sound still hadn't awakened them. I turned back to the figure and slowly stepped out from behind the tree. I crept toward the person, my heart thumping inside my chest. When I was close enough to strike them, I placed the tip of my sword against their back.

"What are you doing?" I asked.

The figure froze and their robe fell to the ground, but there was no one there. I staggered back a few steps in surprise and looked around.

"Did you really think you could sneak up on me?"

I whirled around. An elderly woman stood there with her arms folded across her chest. She had long white hair and wore a collar with clear gemstones. Realization struck me and I recognized her as a member of the Assembly, though I couldn't remember her name.

"I heard a noise and came to investigate," I said. "I wasn't sure who you were or what you were doing."

"You mortals are always trying to interfere with

the business of dragons," the woman said.

"I wasn't—"

"Never mind that. Do you know why you are here?"

"Do you mean why *you* are here?" I asked.

"No."

We stared at each other in silence until it grew awkward.

"I'm sorry, I don't remember your name."

"Tyrval," she said. "I remember yours, Eldwin."

"Why are you here?" I asked.

"Because it was the only way I could reach you. Can you put that blade down?"

I lowered my sword. "Sorry. You came all the way here from the Island of Lost Souls to find me?"

"No, of course not. I've never been on that island."

"Then how did I see you and the others when I was there?" I asked.

"You were brought to us," Tyrval said.

"I'm confused."

"Clearly," Tyrval smirked.

"Funny," I replied. "But I'm serious."

"The Assembly does not reside on the Island of Lost Souls. While you were there, you were brought magically to our domain."

"Where you then severed my bond with Sion," I snapped.

"Yes. Despite our combined knowledge, it is possible that we can make mistakes. We realized that we erred when the Path restored your bond. On behalf of the Assembly, I apologize to you. We were wrong in our judgment."

I wasn't sure if she was lying. She seemed genuine, and she was the only one who had shown any sort of pity toward me when the Assembly voted to revoke my bond.

"I find it hard to believe that you came here just to apologize," I said.

"You are perceptive," Tyrval replied. "No, that's not the only reason. You need to seek out our domain."

"What for?"

"You are trying to track down a wayward dragon soul, yes?"

"How did you know?" I asked.

Tyrval shook her head. "That's not important. Seek out the Assembly. You'll have to sway the others, but there is a way we can help."

"That's good news," I said. "For once."

"Do whatever it takes to find us, Eldwin."

"Why can't you just come here?" I asked.

"Eldwin?"

I turned around at the sound of Maren's voice.

She was standing a few feet away. "What are you doing?"

"I'm talking to Tyrval," I replied, but when I turned back, the old woman was gone.

"Who's Tyrval?"

I frowned and scanned the area, but there was no sign of her. Even the robe that had fallen onto the ground was gone. The only thing that remained was the pile of rocks Tyrval had stacked.

"No one," I answered.

Maren and I walked back to the camp and I saw from my peripheral that Maren kept glancing at me. We reached the camp and I saw that Sion was awake. She looked around curiously.

What is it? I asked.

I felt something, Sion replied. *A presence.* She looked at me. *Did you see anything?*

Yes. It was a woman. Well, a dragon, but in the form of a human. She's a member of the Assembly. Have you heard of it? I asked.

No. What is it?

Supposedly, it's the leadership over dragons. At least, that's what they claim. Are you aware of anything like that? A governing body over your kind?

No, Sion repeated. *I have not been around many dragons, but there was one I knew at Rory's torture place that often spoke of a powerful dragon-god called Brold. His mind was ravaged and he often spoke in circles.*

He wasn't crazy, I said. *Not about Brold, anyway. I've met him. We've got a change of plans. We need to find the Assembly.*

I could feel Sion probing my mind and I removed the mental barrier I'd put up.

"Were you sleepwalking?" Maren suddenly asked.

"I don't think so," I replied. "You're probably going to think I'm crazy, but I was talking to a dragon. Well, a dragon-god. Or something. Anyway, they can help us with Demris."

"Who's they?"

"The Assembly."

Maren stared at me blankly. "And that is … what, exactly?"

"Sorry, it's what the leaders of the dragons call themselves."

"Dragons don't have leaders," Maren said.

"That might not be true," I replied. "One of them was here. She said we need to seek them out. They can help us."

"If they can help, then why haven't they already done so?"

"Your guess is as good as mine," I said. "I tried to ask that, but Tyrval disappeared when you were calling my name. Maybe her magic weakened or something."

"Did you hit your head?" Maren asked. "Maybe we should take you to see a healer."

"I don't need a healer. I need you to trust me."

Maren regarded me for a long moment, then nodded. "You know I do."

"We need to find the Assembly, but Tyrval was less than helpful with how we're supposed to do that. I was hoping Sion knew something, but she knows less than I do."

"Then what do we do?" Maren asked.

"Maybe we can find something in the library at the Citadel?"

"That's too far away. We'll lose Demris's trail again if we leave the area."

I chewed my lower lip in thought. She was right, but what other options did we have? If the Assembly had the power to help stop Demris from killing anyone else, we had to find them.

"The closest school would be Katori's," I said. "We could go there. Maybe her library will have something? She knew about the dracolich, so maybe she'll know about the Assembly, too."

Maren nodded. "Maybe."

I could tell she didn't want to get too far away from Demris, but I wasn't going to leave her out here by herself.

"If Katori doesn't know anything, we'll come back out here until we have something else to go on," I said.

"Promise?"

"I promise, Maren."

"Deal."

We packed up the camp and mounted Sion. The Terranese school was a short distance by dragon back, and we landed outside the walls within an hour. The damage the school had sustained from the battle against the False King's army was almost non-existent now. The gates were open and we walked inside to find the place packed with people. Most of them weren't students, which made me wonder what was going on.

I spotted a familiar face and waved my arms to get his attention. "Domori!"

The warrior stopped when he saw me and offered a low bow. "Eldwin."

"What's going on?" I asked. "I don't remember this many people here last time."

"There's a demon roaming our lands," Domori replied. "It kills innocent people and leaves destruction in its wake. The people have come here for protection."

"A demon? What kind of demon?"

"A demon of green smoke," Domori answered.

3

"You weave an interesting tale, though I have never heard of the Assembly," Katori said thoughtfully.

Maren and I walked with her outside the city walls. Sion had gone to the underground stable and I could feel her contentment through the bond. She was always happiest when she was with me, but being with other dragons took a close second place.

"It makes sense that there would be a hierarchy among dragons," Katori added. "I wonder if they are connected through a bond, something similar to the one we share with them?"

"I don't think so," I replied. "Sion didn't know anything about the Assembly."

Katori stopped walking and stared out at the open field. The tall grass bowed back and forth as a breeze picked up. I wasn't sure if she saw something, and I looked in the same direction. Other than the swaying grass, there was nothing that caught my attention.

"There is a place that might hold some answers," Katori finally said, turning her attention to Maren and me. "I haven't been there since I was a child, but I don't mind taking you there."

"Are you sure?" Maren asked. "We don't want to take you away from your duties."

"It's no trouble," Katori said. "I could use a break from the chaos that has enveloped my school."

"About that," I said, casting a glance at Maren.

"Yes?"

"The demon that your people fear isn't a demon at all."

Katori's eyelids lowered and her gaze burned through me.

"Does this have something to do with the island you visited?" She asked.

"Yes. We brought back a soul with us. It was, uh …"

"It's the soul of my dragon," Maren said. "Since Eldwin's father didn't want to come back, Eldwin let me bring Demris back."

The color in Katori's face disappeared. "A dracolich?"

"No!" Maren replied hurriedly. "It's only his soul. His body is at the Citadel, but he's not traveling there for some reason."

"I think he's looking for something," I said. "He appears to be traveling in a circle and staying in the area."

"I told you it was a bad idea to go there," Katori said. "Nothing good can come from messing with the natural order of things."

"What's done is done," Maren replied. "We

can't change that. But we can find him and stop him from killing more people. Eldwin said the Assembly can help us, so we need to find them."

"I will help you as much as I can, but there is innocent blood on your hands. You will have to deal with that eventually."

Maren didn't say anything.

"Where is this place you mentioned?" I asked, changing the subject.

"A few miles from here. It's an old monastery that rests atop a mountain. The monks who once lived there abandoned the place long ago. My grandfather used to take me there when I was young."

I looked up at the position of the sun, temporarily blinding myself. "Do we have time to get there and back before nightfall?"

"That depends on how long we stay there. We should bring some supplies in case we have to spend the night there."

"How many books are at this monastery?" I asked.

"None."

"Then how exactly are we going to find answers?"

"I said we *might* find answers. The monks had an interesting way of detailing things," Katori said.

"Interesting how?" Maren asked.

"They tattooed their bodies with the knowledge they acquired."

I scrunched my face in disgust. "We're going to see dead bodies?"

"Yes," Katori confirmed. "They don't look dead. At least, not when I saw them last. I believe there was magic keeping them preserved."

"Well then," I said. "Let's get going. The less time we have to spend with corpses, the better."

Within half an hour, we had gathered enough food and water to last until morning and set out for the monastery. Maren and I rode on Sion and Katori took her dragon. As we neared the monastery, Katori's dragon slowed and she motioned for us to land. There was a clearing at the base of the mountain and Sion followed Katori's descent.

Sion landed and I leaped off her back and surveyed the area. A single pathway of worn stone steps led up the mountain to the monastery, which was shrouded in clouds. Katori dismounted and slung a cloth pack over her shoulder.

"Why didn't we just land at the top?" I asked.

"There's a warding spell that prevents dragons from getting near the monastery," Katori replied. "My grandfather told me the monks distrusted dragons, but he didn't know why."

"I don't know how I feel about this now," I said, glancing from the mountaintop to Sion.

"I'm going to leave my dragon here," Katori

said. "If she senses anything, I'll know."

Do you want to stay here? I asked Sion.

No. I will go with you.

"Sion is coming with us," I said. "At least, as far as she can without being stopped by the wards."

"Do you still have the collar I gave you?" Katori asked.

"Yes."

"Good. She'll need to transform to make the climb. The steps are too narrow for her otherwise."

Is that all right with you? I asked Sion.

Yes.

I retrieved the collar from the saddle and put it around Sion's neck. The gemstones glowed and Sion's draconic form slowly melted away until her redheaded human form was all that remained. Just like the last time, she was naked. Maren pulled a robe out from her pack and handed it to me. I helped Sion put it on and she tied the sash around her waist.

I'm ready, she said.

"I think we're all set," I told Katori.

"Good. Follow me and watch where you step. These stones are ancient and likely to break."

"Great," I muttered under my breath.

Katori led the way up the stairway, followed by Maren. I went next and Sion took up the rear. The stones weren't natural formations. They had been carved, though I couldn't tell if it had been done by hand or by magic. The climb up started easily enough, but as we continued higher, the stairway slanted sharply and my leg muscles began to burn.

It's a shame these monks didn't trust dragons, I told Sion. *I'd much rather have flown to the top.*

That makes two of us, Sion replied.

After an hour of climbing, Katori stopped and allowed us to take a break. Maren pulled a canteen from her pack and took a drink, then offered it to me. I accepted it and drank deeply. The cool liquid soothed the dryness in my mouth and I handed the canteen to Sion. She tilted the canteen over and repeatedly flicked her tongue through the water. I tried to hold in my laughter, but it was no use.

Why do you laugh? Sion asked.

I've never seen someone try to drink like that, I replied. *It just looks weird.*

Sion snorted, unamused, and handed the canteen to Maren. I massaged my legs and sat down on one of the stairs to rest.

"We've got to be halfway by now, aren't we?" I asked.

"Not quite," Katori answered. "Closer to a third of the way."

I groaned. Perhaps the privilege of flying had spoiled me. Katori allowed us a few more minutes, then we continued. The climb eventually became dangerous. The stone stairs had been damaged from the elements and were covered with visible cracks. Some stairs were missing large chunks and there were a few times I heard splitting sounds as we climbed.

By the time we reached the top, my legs were trembling and I thought for sure I would collapse in exhaustion. Sion didn't seem tired at all, but Katori and Maren looked as bad as I felt. They were both sweating and breathing heavily. Thankfully, the air this high up was cooler. It was also thinner, so it took a little longer to catch my breath.

I turned my attention to the monastery. It was a huge square structure built of limestone and the entire building had a muddy hue. The elements had damaged parts of the monastery's walls, and some sections were nothing more than a pile of rubble. Moss covered the stones at the base of the structure and looked like it was slowing devouring the monastery from the ground up.

"There is more damage than I remember," Katori remarked.

Multiple stain-glass windows lined the walls on either side of the main entrance and were surprisingly intact, if not overly dirty.

"It's a marvel that anyone was been able to build something this massive up here," I said. "Especially if they didn't trust dragons. How else would they have gotten all their supplies up here?"

"It is curious, isn't it?" Katori replied. "Why build anything this far above civilization?

Regardless, I'm sure they employed magic. That's the only explanation I can come up with."

That made sense, but why the monks built their monastery upon a mountain was a mystery we would probably never know the answer to.

"It took us longer to make the climb than I expected, so we should probably hurry with our search," Katori said. "Judging by the outside appearance, I'm sure the inside is just as bad. I'd rather not have to spend the night here if it isn't necessary."

"I couldn't agree more," Maren said.

We headed for the entrance and I noticed that Sion wasn't following us. I had almost forgotten about the wards. I walked over to her and removed the collar. She transformed back into her draconic form and stretched her wings.

We'll try to be quick, I said.

Please do, Sion replied. *This place makes me uncomfortable.*

4

The interior of the monastery was dark and musky. Katori whispered a spell and a ball of light formed overhead. It illuminated a square room lined with dilapidated wooden benches. On the far left, there was a statue of a hooded monk that had its hands pressed together in a pose of prayer.

"I'm surprised the inside isn't worse," Maren said. Her voice echoed eerily off the walls.

I ignored the shiver that ran down my spine and walked over to the statue to inspect it. The monk's face was missing, but I couldn't tell if that was due to damage or if it had been sculpted without one. A large silver bowl sat at the feet of the statue and it looked like there was dried blood in the bottom.

There was something else, too. I knelt and peered closer. It was difficult to tell what the item was.

"Can you bring that light over here?" I asked.

Katori obliged and the sphere floated closer. The item was covered in dried blood, but the light clearly revealed what it was. A dragon scale. I pried it free from the bowl and brushed off the grossness with my hand. Its copper surface shimmered under the magical light.

"I didn't know there were copper dragons," I said as I stood up.

"There aren't," Maren replied.

"Then explain this." I tossed the scale at her.

She caught it and scrunched her face in confusion. Katori stepped closer to take a look and her reaction was similar to Maren's.

"I've never seen a metallic dragon," Katori said. "This scale, if it's really from a dragon, would suggest that they exist."

"Or maybe they did in the past," Maren suggested. "How old did you say this monastery is?"

"I'm not sure," Katori said. "Two or three hundred years, maybe. It was here before the school. I know that for certain. There's at least one book in the school's library that references the monastery's location and it was written twenty years before my people began constructing the school."

Maren offered the scale back to me.

"Can you put it in your pack?" I asked. "It's too big for my coin purse."

"This scale does seem smaller than normal," Maren said.

"That's because it was probably from a hatchling," Katori replied. "As dragons grow, their scales get bigger and thicker."

So far, this place had added more questions and given no answers. I glanced around and spotted an archway that led into another room.

"What's in there? The bodies?" I asked.

"Yes, if I remember correctly." Katori offered a pleasant smile, but it did little to ease my disgust. She and Maren entered the next room and I slowly followed. Debris littered the floor and it was covered with a thick layer of grime. A hearth roughly six feet long was built into one of the walls and displayed above it was three glass cases. Each one contained the body of a man covered in tattoos.

"That glass is the cleanest thing in this place," Maren said.

She was right. The glass was completely clear, giving us a perfect view of the bodies. The tattoos were all inked in black and they covered every inch of visible skin. There were some pictures, but there were mostly words in a curvy script that I couldn't decipher.

"Is that Terranese?" I asked.

"Yes and no," Katori said. "It's very similar, but there are some letters that I don't know."

"Is there anyone you know who can translate it?" The idea that we might have found a clue about where to find the Assembly and not be able to decipher it was frustrating.

"We have many diverse students, so there might be someone at the school who can read it."

"These cases look too heavy to move," Maren said. "Should we take one of the bodies with us?"

"I would never dare to disrespect the dead in

such a way," Katori replied.

"I'm sorry, I didn't mean to offend you." Maren stared at the body and shrugged. "The only other option is to bring someone here, but it took hours to climb that path."

"We have time," Katori said.

"Not if you want to avoid more bodies," I replied. "The longer it takes to find the Assembly, the more time Demris has to cause destruction."

"Yes, I am aware."

Katori clasped her hands behind her back and moved away from the coffins.

"Do what you must, but I will not be a part of this desecration."

Maren and I exchanged looks, then began searching for a way to open the glass without having to break it. On each corner of the outward-facing pane, there were small runes etched into the glass. Maren pressed one and it glowed faintly. We pressed the others and the glass pane came loose and crashed to the floor. The pane shattered and sent shards flying everywhere.

"Sorry," I mouthed to Katori, who had a horrified expression plastered across her face.

I looked at the body and watched in surprise as it deteriorated and crumbled into a pile of dirt. "What just happened?"

"There was a preservation spell on the coffin," Maren said. "It didn't break when the glass came off, though. I'm not sure why it failed."

Katori kept her distance but offered her thoughts. "It was likely that another spell was triggered to prevent the theft of the body. I hadn't considered it before, but it makes sense that the monks wouldn't want their knowledge stolen."

"So, we're back to having to bring someone up here," I groaned.

"We can stay here and keep searching while you return to the school," Maren said to Katori. "We've got enough supplies to last us a day or two."

As much as I wanted to find the Assembly and stop Demris, I didn't like the idea of spending the night in the creepy monastery. I almost opened my mouth to say that when Katori agreed.

"Fine. I expect to find both of you alive when I return. Don't disappoint me."

"I don't plan on dying in here, trust me," I said.

We followed Katori through the monastery and back outside. Sion was waiting near the top of the stairs, her boredom apparent.

"Do you want Sion to take you down to the bottom?" I asked.

"No need," Katori replied. She put her lips together and whistled a short pattern.

I looked at Maren but she shrugged in reply.

"I'll be back as quickly as I can. And try not to touch anything. There's no telling what this place holds."

Katori walked to the edge of the monastery grounds where a short wall was the only thing between her and a hundred-foot drop. She peered over and watched silently, then leaped over the side. Maren gasped and my mouth dropped open. We rushed over to the wall and looked down just in time to see Katori's wingless dragon swoop underneath and safely catch her.

"That was insane!" I shouted. "I don't know if I would try it, though."

I'd prefer you didn't, Sion said.

Sometimes you are no fun, I replied jokingly.

"Let's get back inside and see what else we can find," Maren said, walking back towards the monastery. "You can do life-threatening tricks later."

I smirked as I followed her back into the building. The magical ball of light Katori had conjured was gone, so Maren created her own and we went back into the room with the bodies where Maren examined the empty coffin.

"Three bodies can't contain much knowledge," I said. "It seems like there should be more somewhere. I'm going to look around." I was trying to sound brave and hoped Maren would dissuade me, but instead, she waved me off.

"Scream like a girl if you need anything," she laughed.

I shook my head and wandered into the next room. It was empty with no access anywhere else.

A single window provided enough natural light to fill the entire room. There wasn't much to see besides dust. I was about to leave when I stumbled over a rug. It was almost indistinguishable from the dark grime on the floor. The corner that I stumbled on was curled up, revealing clean woodwork underneath.

I think there's a hidden door here, I told Sion.

Where does it go?

Down. It's in the floor.

I grabbed the corner of the rug and pulled it back. I was right. There was a rectangular wooden door with a bronze pull handle. A casual tug didn't accomplish anything, so I used both hands and heaved as hard as I could. The door came loose and the hinges creaked as it opened.

"Maren! You should come and see this!"

"What is it?" Her voice echoed into the chamber.

"A door to a hidden room!"

"I'll be there in a minute."

She didn't sound as excited as I felt. I shrugged and looked inside, expecting it to be pitch black. Instead, the room was well-lit by windows. A wooden ladder led down into the room. Unlike the rest of the place, there were no signs of disrepair. I climbed down the ladder with careful steps just in case the wood was decayed, but it was sturdy.

I reached the bottom and looked around. The

room appeared to have once been a study. Leather bound books lined the walls and there was a writing desk next to a hearth, though this one was much smaller than the one upstairs.

There were two doors, one on each end of the chamber, and one of them was ajar. I walked over and pushed it fully open, then paused in confusion.

Someone was whispering inside the room.

5

I drew my sword and stepped into the room.

The light from the windows behind me poured into the chamber, which was small and rectangular. There was no one inside, though, which I found strange. Where had the person that'd been whispering gone?

What's happening? Sion asked. *I sense ... something. I don't know what it is.*

There's nothing, I replied. *I heard whispering, but there's no one in here. It's the strangest thi—*

The whispering started again. It was coming from the end of the room. I followed the sound and stopped at a wooden chest banded with steel. Its lid was open and propped against the wall behind it. I sheathed my blade and stepped closer to peer inside.

A glittering blue gemstone caught my attention. Multicolored wisps swirled within it, weaving a lethargic pattern. The stone was set in the hilt of a short sword that was forged of bronze. The whispering grew in intensity as I reached for the hilt. When my fingers were within an inch of touching the metal surface, the whispering ceased.

I grabbed ahold of the sword and pulled it out of the chest. My mind suddenly became focused and strength spread throughout my limbs. It was rejuvenating. I swung the sword a few times. It was perfectly weighted and barely seemed to take any effort to wield it.

The wall to my left glittered with numerous colors and I realized that the room was an armory. Every weapon had a gemstone like the sword I held, though the gems varied in size and color. Sion's uneasiness filtered through the bond.

Everything is fine, I said. *It's an armory. I guess I must have been hearing things because there's no one in here.*

Be wary, Sion warned. *There is something there, whether you can see it or not.*

I looked around the room again but there was nothing to cause concern. Yet if Sion felt there was something amiss, I knew better than to ignore her. I exited the room and closed the door, then climbed back up the stairs to show Maren the blade I had found. She stepped into the doorway suddenly and startled me.

"Gods!" I cursed. "You move around like a mouse."

"You're not scared of the dark, are you?" She asked.

"Hardly. Anyway, look what I found."

I held the sword up. Maren gazed at the blade and nodded appreciatively. "That's nice craftsmanship. That topaz is an added touch, too."

"Tell me about it. It's so light, I can barely tell I'm even holding it."

"Where did you find it?" Maren asked.

"Downstairs. Come on, I'll show you."

I led her down the trap door and showed her the armory.

"This place is full of surprises," Maren said. "These weapons have got to be worth a small fortune. The gemstones alone are worth more than some nobles I know."

"That's what I was thinking," I said. "I'm sure we could easily sell these."

"Well, we aren't taking them without Katori's permission. This monastery is Terranese property, and I think she should decide what to do with it all. What's in the other room?"

I shrugged. "I didn't get that far."

"Let's find out, then."

Maren led the way from the armory to the other door. When she tried to turn the handle, it didn't budge.

"It's locked," she said, frowning.

"Maybe there's a key," I replied, glancing at the desk. I set the sword down and examined the contents of the drawers and found one hidden beneath some blank parchments. "Try this one." I tossed the key to Maren and she caught it, then slid it into the handle. She turned the key and there was a click.

We exchanged looks and Maren opened the door. It swung open on silent hinges. I moved to stand behind Maren and peered over her shoulder.

There was a stairway that led down into darkness.

"Shall we?" Maren asked.

"Not without some light," I answered.

Maren conjured another ball of floating light and we descended the stairs. It was a longer trip down than I expected and it made me wonder just how far down into the mountain the monks had built their monastery—and why. When we finally reached the bottom, I couldn't see the doorway we'd entered through even with Maren's magic.

"How deep do you think we are?" I asked.

"There's no telling," Maren said. "But we must be pretty far down. I lost count of the stairs close to two hundred."

Maren closed her eyes and whispered a few words and the sphere of light expanded, banishing more of the darkness. The shadows parted to reveal an archway that led into another chamber. We stepped under the arch and the sphere illuminated dozens of glass coffins lining the walls. They were filled with bodies like the ones aboveground.

"There's so many," Maren whispered.

"Maybe the monks didn't abandon the monastery, maybe they all just died off," I said.

I walked closer to one of the coffins and looked at the tattoos that covered the body inside. They were similar in style to the ones on the bodies upstairs.

"Katori's translator is going to be busy. Looks

like we should prepare to spend a day or two here," I said.

Maren stood beside me and frowned. "We're going to lose Demris."

"We'll find him again if we do," I replied. "He hasn't gone far. And besides, this place might have the guidance we need to find the Assembly."

"How do we even know that the Assembly can help us?"

"I don't *know,* but I don't see why Tyrval would lie about it." I turned away from the coffins and looked at Maren. "Can we go back upstairs? This place makes me uncomfortable."

"I thought you said you weren't afraid of the dark?" Maren giggled.

"You're hilarious," I replied, rolling my eyes.

"I know."

I couldn't help but smile. We headed back up the stairs, which ended up being much harder than coming down had been. When we stepped into the study, I heard the whispering again and looked at the desk. I'd forgotten that I'd left the bronze sword there. I retrieved it and brought it with me to the main level of the monastery.

"Katori's been gone a while now," Maren said.

She was right. The sun was beginning to set. I sighed with the realization that we were going to be forced into spending the night in the monastery.

"I'm sure she isn't going to make the trek up

here in the dark, so we'd better get a fire going and settle in for the night."

"If you get scared, just let me know," Maren laughed. "I'll hold you."

"Whatever." I shook my head at her and walked into the room with the pews. The long benches were all ruined, but I grabbed the one I thought was the worst and used the bronze sword to hack it into smaller pieces for a fire.

I was about to carry some of the pieces outside when I heard the rumble of thunder in the distance.

"Great," I muttered. "What else could go wrong?"

We're going to spend the night here, I told Sion. *You might want to find shelter in case it rains.*

I saw a cave on the way up, Sion answered. *I'll stay there.*

Do you want me to put the collar back on?

No, I am fine for now.

I found a spot that was a decent distance from anything else that could catch on fire and placed a few pieces of wood together.

"Would you mind using your magic to start the fire?" I asked Maren.

"Sure," she replied.

Once the fire was going, I stacked the rest of the wood in a pile and brushed a space on the floor clear of debris, then laid down. It wasn't very comfortable, but it was better than sleeping in the rain. I rolled onto my side to face the fire and watched the flames reflect off the blade's shiny surface.

Eventually, my eyes grew heavy. I tried to stay awake but it was no use, so I gave in to the darkness. My dreams were confusing and filled with whispers. After a traumatic nightmare, I woke up drenched in sweat. Maren was asleep on the other side of the fire, curled into a ball. I got up and added some wood to the fire, then I heard the whispering again.

The sword was calling to me. There was no doubt in my mind this time. I guessed the gemstone was enchanted and the whispering I heard was the call of the magic. It wanted to be used, *needed* to be used. That was the blade's purpose. To be wielded. I picked the sword up and studied the swirling colors within the gem.

It had been too long since the blade had been cast aside. Its purpose wasn't being fulfilled, and the magic cried out to me for a solution. My grip tightened on the hilt and I looked at Maren's motionless form. She was still asleep. That was good. She wouldn't be able to stop me. I walked out of the monastery and looked for Sion.

The blade needed to be used.

6

The wind howled as I stalked through the rain. Sion had mentioned a cave, but I was having trouble finding it. Water dripped down my face and into my eyes, but I ignored the sting. The blade's cries were deafening now and I was focused solely on appeasing it.

A flash of lightning briefly lit up the sky and a few moments later thunder cracked loudly. The fleeting light had revealed a cave entrance ahead. I tightened my grip on the blade and I felt like my steps were being directed by someone else.

Eldwin? Sion's voice sleepily drifted into my mind.

I'm coming, I replied.

My heart was hammering in my chest. The magic of the sword rippled along my arm, giving me goosebumps. I closed the distance to the cave and stepped inside. It was pitch black, but I could see Sion's glowing eyes. She was watching me and I could feel her curiosity through the bond.

What is it? Sion asked.

The sword forced me to keep silent and I suddenly realized what was happening. The sword wanted me to kill Sion. I tried to fight it, but I had let my guard down and the magic was in control. I sprinted toward Sion and lifted the blade to strike her.

Sion roared and backed away but refused to attack me. I felt guilty for listening to the sword, but I couldn't stop my body. The gemstone flared with a burst of blue light and I was able to see clearly in the darkness. Sion's tail flicked back and forth behind her. Her teeth were bared and she looked ferocious, but there was a hint of fear in the bond.

What are you doing? She asked.

I ... can't ... stop it, I managed to tell her before I rushed forward again. I swung the blade in a left and right looping motion, forming an 'X' pattern in the air. Sion tried to back up again, but she reached the end of the cave. I aimed for the upper part of her neck and swung with all my might.

Sion's tail suddenly filled my vision as it slammed into me, sending me crashing into the wall. I managed to keep my grip on the blade and rose to my feet. Before I could fully gain my balance, Sion dashed past me and out of the cave. I hurried after her, the sword demanding her blood.

Rain and wind lashed my face but the blade would not submit. Sion kept her distance, but she was ready to take me down. Her anger melded with her confusion and I tried to tell her to flee, but I couldn't force the words through the bond.

The gemstone flared again, and this time a bolt of jagged lightning arced from the pommel and struck Sion in the chest. It must have drained her strength because she collapsed onto the ground. She was conscious and her eyes were fixed on me as I approached her. I shook my head in denial, but the sword's magic was too strong to overcome.

I stood over Sion and raised the blade above my head. It was time. Time to let the sword bask in the blood of dragons again. Time to unleash its dark fury upon the land. I tried to close my eyes as I swung the blade downward but the sword wouldn't let me.

Something struck the blade and it was ripped from my grasp. It clanged onto the stones behind me and I heard the whispering again. It was frantic, demanding that I pick it up. Now that I wasn't holding the weapon, it was easier to fight the pull.

"What are you doing?" Maren screamed at me.

She ran to Sion and looked her over, then turned to me. I hadn't seen Maren this angry since the day Jon had attacked me at the Citadel.

"Answer me!" She demanded.

"I don't know!" I shouted back. "I don't know what came over me. It's the sword. The sword ..." I looked over my shoulder and spotted the blade.

Maren pushed past me and struck me in the chest with her fist. I rubbed the spot and watched her walk over to the blade. She knelt and inspected it but didn't touch it. I walked over but stopped a few feet away.

"It's the gemstone," Maren said. "The magic imbued within it is dark and ugly. No wonder you tried to kill your dragon."

Shame washed over me and I went back over to

Sion. I lowered myself to my knees and laid my head against Sion's.

I'm sorry, I said. *That wasn't me.*

I know, Sion replied. *That's why I didn't bite your head off your body.*

Despite the gravity of the situation, I laughed. Tears welled in my eyes and one streamed down my cheek, but it was quickly washed away by the rain.

I told you I sensed something in that armory. You didn't listen.

I'm sorry, I repeated. *I didn't see anything in there. I didn't realize it was the weapons themselves.*

Not all threats are visible, Sion said.

That was a hard lesson to learn. If it wasn't for Maren, I don't know what I would have done.

Sion didn't reply. I caressed her scaly neck for a moment, then rose to my feet.

Are you all right? Can you move?

I am fine, Sion replied. *I just need to gather my strength.*

Maren approached, carrying the sword by the blade. She walked to the edge of the cliff and hurled the sword off the side. Relief washed over me at the knowledge that the blade was far away from me.

"That sword was cursed," Maren said as she joined us.

"I think it's safe to assume the other weapons in

that room were designed the same way."

"Did the sword want you to kill a dragon specifically?" Maren asked.

"Yes," I replied.

"These monks weren't spiritual people." Maren looked from Sion to me. "They were a cult of dragon slayers."

"Dragon slayers?" I asked incredulously. "This close to the Terranese school?"

"Remember what Katori said? The monastery was here long before the school was. The monks must have vanished before the riders had a foothold here."

I considered what Maren said and had to agree. Who else would forge weapons designed to kill dragons?

"We need to destroy those weapons," I said.

"I'm not sure that's easily done. We'll tell Katori and let her decide what to do with them. We have enough problems of our own."

"Fair enough."

The storm wasn't letting up. My clothes were soaked and I wanted nothing more than to get warm by the fire, but I didn't want to leave Sion in the rain by herself.

Go, Sion said. *I'll be fine.*

No, I replied. *I'm not leaving you.*

Sion didn't argue, which told me that she didn't

want to be alone.

"I'm going to stay with Sion until she can get into the cave," I told Maren. "You should go back into the monastery."

Maren seemed hesitant, but she finally nodded and left. I sat down next to Sion and leaned against her. Despite the wind and rain, her body was warm. She brought her right wing up and stretched it out over our heads. The rain pattered against the membrane but we were sheltered beneath it.

I'm afraid that Maren will be broken if we can't get Demris back to his body, I said.

I think your fear is justified.

I don't know what to do, I sighed.

You'll figure it out. You always do.

I wasn't sure how Sion assumed that. I felt like things just continued to happen to me and despite my best efforts, they never went the way I wanted.

I hope these insane monks knew where the Assembly was located. If we can find them, I'm confident that they'll help us.

Let it be so, Sion replied. *I'm ready to get out of the rain.*

Sion tucked her wing back and stood up. She heaved in a deep breath and walked toward the cave. I followed beside her and paused at the cave's entrance as she disappeared inside. I stood there in the rain until I was certain Sion was resting, then I headed back to the monastery.

Maren was still awake and sitting beside the fire. I sat down beside her and stared into the flames. We sat quietly for a long while, but Maren eventually grabbed my hand and squeezed it.

"I'm sorry I yelled at you," she whispered.

"Don't be," I replied. "I deserved it."

"You couldn't have known that sword would take control of you like that."

"I know, but … still. Thank you for stopping me. You're always there when I need you. I hope that never changes."

"I don't plan on that changing," Maren replied.

I wrapped my arm around her shoulder and hugged her close. She leaned her head against mine and we stayed like that for a long while.

7

I awoke to the sound of voices.

It was morning and Katori had returned. She was discussing something with Maren, but I wasn't able to make out what they were saying. I stretched and wiped the sleep from my eyes, then put my boots on and walked outside.

Katori glanced at me briefly but kept her attention on Maren. Standing with them was an elderly man. He was bald, but his beard was long and white, flowing down to the middle of his chest. His eyebrows were thick and bushy, making it appear as though he had two large hairy caterpillars on his face. Maren finished speaking and Katori smiled at me.

"Sleep well?" She asked.

"Not really," I replied. "I assume Maren told you what happened with the sword I found?"

Katori nodded solemnly. "I am saddened to hear what nearly happened. How are you feeling? Can you still hear the sword whispering to you?"

"No. After Maren threw it off the cliff, I haven't heard it since."

"Good. That answers one of my questions." Katori motioned toward the old man. "This is Yoshino. He can interpret the ancient Terranese on the bodies. I apologize for not returning last night.

By the time I found him, it was too dark to make the trip back up here. We left before dawn to get here as early as possible."

"We appreciate it," I said, then looked at Maren. "Did you tell her about the other bodies?"

"Not yet," Maren answered.

"There are more?" Katori asked. "Where?"

"The main area up here is only a small part of the monastery. There's a trapdoor that leads down into the mountain and there's a huge room full of coffins," I said.

"It's a mausoleum," Maren clarified. "And it's enormous, but there are only about fifty coffins with bodies in them. The rest are empty."

"That is interesting," Katori said. "Let us go and see it. Yoshino wants to be home to his wife by dinner."

"Sounds like a plan to me," I said.

We stopped in the room that had the three coffins and Yoshino spent some time reading the tattoos of the two remaining bodies. I was anxious to get down to the other bodies because I had a feeling there would be more valuable information on them considering where they were hidden.

"What do they say?" Maren asked. "The tattoos, I mean."

Yoshino spoke in a different language to Katori. She listened intently and responded in the same language a few times. I assumed she was asking questions. Finally, she nodded and turned to me and Maren.

"He says these bodies are like welcome signs to their brethren. Their tattoos say this place is a sanctum for dragon hunters."

"I knew it!" Maren said. "These monks were dragon slayers."

"So it would seem," Katori replied.

I led everyone to the room with the trapdoor and we climbed down the ladder one at a time. I opened the door to the armory to show Katori the treasure trove that was inside. I didn't step past the threshold, though. My fear that I would hear the other weapons whispering to me kept me at bay, but thankfully there was nothing but silence.

"It's a pity these weapons were forged to kill dragons," Katori said. "They are beautiful and would sell for a high price."

"That's what I was thinking, too," I said.

Katori shook her head. "They are too dangerous to let loose into the world. I think they should stay hidden in here, protected in secrecy."

"It would probably be a good idea to add warding spells on the door," Maren said. "Just in case someone happens to find the trapdoor."

"That is a good idea," Katori replied. "I will take care of that later. Where are the other bodies?"

Maren opened the door that led to the mausoleum and conjured a ball of magical light.

"They're down here. There's a lot of stairs," she warned.

"Yoshino is in good health," Katori said. "His age hides his fortitude."

Maren's facial expression showed her doubt, but she didn't say anything. She went first, followed by Katori and Yoshino. I went last and was surprised when Yoshino made it to the bottom and didn't even seem winded. My legs burned from the exertion and I had to pause for a moment before I could follow the others into the mausoleum.

"This place must have taken many years to build," Katori said with wonder. "The ceiling is lost to shadow high above."

"It is *very* impressive," I said. "Just think about what they could have accomplished if they hadn't been focused on killing dragons."

Yoshino said something to Katori and walked over to one of the coffins. Katori whispered the words to a spell and a ball of light similar to Maren's came into existence. It hovered next to the old man and he began relaying the information of the tattoos to Katori. Once he stopped talking, Katori translated.

"Yoshino says the monks were on a spiritual mission to expel dragons from the world. They crafted spells and weapons that were able to penetrate the scales of dragons and killed many of them. Most of the tattoos explain how they crafted their weapons."

Yoshino went from body to body, explaining the knowledge that was inked into their skin. There was a lot of information about the monks themselves, but nothing about the Assembly or where to find them. As Yoshino got down to the last two bodies, I started to fear that this had been a waste of time.

We're not any closer to finding the Assembly, I told Sion.

I'm sure that is disappointing to you, she replied.

How are you feeling? Did that spell from the sword cause any damage?

There is no lasting damage. There is a little pain that remains, but I feel it quickly fading.

Good, I said. *I'm sorry again for what happened.*

You have apologized many times for something that was not your fault, Sion said. *What must I do for you to understand that I do not hold any ill will toward you?*

I smiled, relieved that she truly wasn't angry with me. I knew she was right, but I couldn't help feeling bad about it.

I'll try to stop thinking about it, I promised her.

Good.

My attention turned to Katori when I heard the word Assembly.

"What did you say?" I asked. "I'm sorry, I was talking with Sion."

"The monks were trying to find something they called the Assembly of Dragon Gods. They believed that if they killed off the leaders of the dragons, then the rest of them would also die. That doesn't sound logical to me, but who knows what they were thinking?"

"The Assembly!" I said excitedly. "That's what we're looking for. Where is it?"

Katori asked Yoshino and the old man continued translating the tattoos.

"He says the monks couldn't find the location, but they believe that's because the Assembly moved their fortress around magically."

"I'm glad these crazy people weren't able to find the Assembly and potentially kill off all the dragons," Maren said.

"Me too," I replied.

"Are there any clues as to where they believe the fortress might have been? I mean, I guess it's possible the Assembly moved their fortress around magically, but what places did they move it to?"

Yoshino moved to the last body and said something to Katori.

"He says there's a map."

Maren and I crowded the old man trying to see it. There was a general outline of the land on the monk's chest, along with some identifiable landmarks. Tiny stars dotted the map randomly.

"What do these represent?" I asked, pointing at

the stars.

Katori asked Yoshino and he squinted at the tattoos under the map, then replied to her.

"The monks were certain those were spots where the Assembly moved their fortress. Yoshino says the Assembly moved from location to location, always evading the monks. That's it. That's everything."

I looked at Maren. We stared at each other in silence, but I knew we were thinking the same thing.

"We need to go to these locations," I said. Maren nodded in agreement. "There's just one problem. How do we take this map with us? When we opened the other coffin, the body disintegrated."

"I can help with that," Katori said. "I'll need a parchment, but I can make a copy of the map so we don't lose any more knowledge."

"There are a few pieces up in the study," I said.

"Bring me one," Katori instructed.

I heaved a sigh and did as she asked. I had wrongfully assumed I was in decent shape, and this proved to be true as I had to stop countless times going up the stairs, as well as back down. When I handed the parchment to Katori, I thought for sure my legs were going to give out on me, especially since we still had to go back up to leave the monastery.

Katori placed the parchment against the glass

and lined it up with the outline on the monk's chest, then closed her eyes and spoke a few words of magic. A glowing red line appeared on the parchment and it traced out the details of the map. When Katori handed it to me, I saw the lines had been burned into the parchment.

"Thank you," I said.

"Find the Assembly and stop Demris," Katori said. "Innocent people are dying for no reason."

"We will," Maren said.

I looked over the map and pointed to one of the stars. "We'll start here," I said. It was a place I had been before, a bittersweet place.

It was the Necra Desert.

8

The Necra Desert was just as I remembered.

Scorching, lifeless, and endless rolling hills of sand. Looking back, it was a wonder that any of Rory's crew had survived the place after I'd left. This was where Sion and I had found each other, where our bonding had happened. It seemed so long ago, years even, yet it had only been months.

We'd spent the entire previous day searching the desert for the location on the map, but we'd had little luck. Maren and I spent the night beside Sion, cuddling for warmth against the cold that darkness brought. We got up early and hit the sky, spending the last few hours looking for something other than sand.

"This is pointless!" Maren yelled from behind me.

I glanced over my shoulder at her. Her face was flushed red and she was sweating. I had noticed that her fiery temperament was worst when she was either hungry or tired. Judging by the look on her face, I guessed she was both.

Find a spot to land, I told Sion. *We need to take a break.*

I thought you'd never ask, Sion replied. She swooped down and gradually descended until she landed gently atop one of the many dunes. It was nearly midday and there wasn't a cloud in the sky, which made flying around under the sun miserable. I could understand Maren's discomfort, but it seemed to be taking a harder toll on her.

Maren retrieved a canteen from her bag and drank deeply, then sat down in the sand. I sat beside her and flinched as the heat from the sand penetrated my clothes. This had to be the most terrible place in existence. Well, aside from the Island of Lost Souls.

"I don't think we're going to find anything," Maren groaned. "We've lost time and now who knows where Demris is or what he's done."

I let her vent and didn't say anything.

How are you doing? I asked Sion. She was able to go longer without water than humans, but she still needed to stay hydrated.

I'm fine for now, but my wings grow weary of flying.

I pulled the map out from my bag and unfolded it. Based on the few landmarks we'd encountered, I knew we were in the general area of where we should be looking.

"Maybe the wind has covered the place with sand," I said.

"And maybe it doesn't even exist. Maybe the monks were liars on top of being dragon killers."

I smiled at Maren's snappy reply, but I was growing frustrated as well. My logic in coming to the desert first was that I assumed it would be the hardest place to find any clues, and I'd been correct. That did little to bolster my flagging morale, though. Despite all that, I was trying to keep a positive attitude, but Maren was quickly making that difficult.

Sion perked her head up and tilted it to the side.

Do you hear anything? I asked her.

No, but I feel something. There's magic pulsing, but it's faint.

Where?

Sion closed her eyes and was silent for a long moment.

Over the hill, she replied. *At the bottom, I think. It's difficult to tell.*

I put the map away and stood up, then marched across the sand. The hill drifted down progressively which made it easy to navigate. Sion and Maren stayed behind, but Sion stood at the top of the dune, watching over me protectively.

Be careful, she warned.

Is there something dangerous down here?

Magic is always dangerous, Sion replied.

I wiped the sweat from my forehead and continued down to the bottom of the hill. The landscape leveled out, but I didn't see anything. Well, other than sand. I kicked the ground in aggravation and stubbed my toes on something hard under the sand. I gritted my teeth through the pain and went down on one knee to investigate.

A few inches under the sand, there was stone. I used my hands to push the sand away and realized it wasn't a small loose stone, it was massive.

"Maren!" I shouted, hoping she could hear me.

Can you two get down here? I asked Sion. *I found something.*

A moment later, Sion landed a few yards away with Maren astride her back. I waved Maren to come near and continued pushing the sand away from the stone.

"There's something under the sand," I said.

"It's going to take you too long to dig it out. Move."

I did as Maren asked and moved over by Sion. Maren traced some runes into the sand, then stepped back and closed her eyes. She whispered a spell and the runes began to glow. At first, nothing happened. Then the sand began to lift into the air, slowly revealing the stone beneath. It wasn't a boulder, as I had assumed, but it was an enormous stone foundation. Judging by the distinct shape, it wasn't a natural formation.

That's what I sensed, Sion said.

"Sion said this thing is pulsing with magic," I told Maren.

"Yes, but it's weak. That's probably because it hasn't been used for a long time."

"Is there any way to tell what the magic's purpose is?" I asked.

"Maybe." Maren closed her eyes and for the next several minutes, everything was silent. I stared at the sand that floated above us, suspended in place. Magic was such a mysterious power to me. It had limits, of course, but based on what I had seen so far it was difficult to imagine what those limits were.

"The magic is tethered to another location," Maren said as she opened her eyes. "I'm not sure what this place was used for, but since it is connected to something else, I think we are on the right track."

"It seems logical that this might have been one of the places the Assembly used to move their fortress to. Can you track where the magic is connected?"

"It'll be difficult, but it's not impossible," Maren replied.

"All you can do is try," I said. "Since we've finally found a clue that can lead us to the Assembly, we need to follow it."

"I know. I just want to find Demris and get him back to his body. I'm ready for all of this to be over."

Over the next several days, Sion flew in the direction that Maren directed as she tracked the course of the magic. It took us far to the south, past the Terranese school, and along the coast. We flew over the area where the ferryman's boat had tipped over, but there was no sign of his body or the boat.

I wondered briefly who would ferry the wayward souls to the island now that the ferryman was dead. My curiosity made me want to pose the question to Maren, but I knew it probably wasn't something she wanted to talk about yet.

The magic led us to a stone foundation identical to the one in the desert, but this one was offshore. The dark blue water hid it from view, but it was in an isolated area too small for large ships. Just as before, there was nothing but the foundation and a weak pulse of magic. Maren continued to track the magic, which turned us to the east, toward the heart of Osnen.

We stopped to rest at a town on the border of the Terranese lands and heard stories of demon attacks being told. Maren and I kept to ourselves, but we listened to them all and I could see the worry in Maren's eyes.

The next morning, we headed out before the sun had risen and continued east. Sion didn't complain about the amount of flying she was doing, but I knew she was tired. I took the time to rub her neck comfortingly as we flew, and when we were on the ground to rest, I massaged her wings. The days began to blur like the scenery that passed below us, but we finally crossed into the heartland of Osnen.

The city that served as the capital of the kingdom was bigger than any place I'd ever seen. It was a sprawling metropolis that spread across miles of land. Outside the city proper was farmland, with a multitude of different crops and animals being tended for the sole purpose of feeding the enormous population.

"It's beautiful!" I shouted to Maren. "Should we stop here?"

"No," Maren replied, drawing close to speak into my ear. "I'd rather avoid the place, if possible."

Sion flew over the city and we were just about to clear it when a group of riders launched into the sky and headed straight for us. I figured they were probably curious about who we were and why we were flying over the city, so I wasn't worried as their squad surrounded us. A man in brilliantly polished armor rode a sleek but muscular blue dragon. He glided into position next to Sion and looked at me, then motioned for us to land.

Take us down, I told Sion.

We landed in an open field, and the entire squad of riders followed, landing in a pattern that was intended to dissuade us from flying off. I assumed the show of force was meant to scare anyone with nefarious purposes, but what dragon rider would be up to trouble? Especially this close to the king's domain?

"Identify yourself," the man who had ordered me to land said. He dismounted and approached Sion without any hesitation.

"Eldwin Baines," I said.

"Where are you headed?"

"East," I answered. I figured the less information I divulged, the better off we'd be.

The man looked at Maren and he stood in silence for a moment, then looked back at me.

"Who's the girl?"

"My friend and fellow rider," I replied.

"Her name?" The man asked sternly.

"I am Maren Toft," Maren said. "Unless you have a specific reason for stopping us, we're traveling on important business."

The man shielded his face from the sun and looked at Maren again.

"Princess Maren," he greeted. "My apologies, I didn't recognize you."

"Don't worry about it. I appreciate you doing your duty, but as I mentioned, we must be going."

"I'm afraid that isn't possible, Your Majesty. Your father has been looking for you and we've been instructed to bring you to him if we see you."

"I don't care what my father says," Maren retorted. "I'm leaving."

The man looked at his fellow riders and shook his head slightly.

"You're not going anywhere except to see your father."

"Let's just do what they're asking," I said to Maren. "See your father and let him know you're all right. It sounds like he's just worried about you."

"You don't know him like I do," Maren said.

"Maybe so, but I'd rather not have to flee from a group of armed men."

Maren huffed rebelliously, but she nodded. "Fine."

9

The king's guards accompanied us back to the city and I was forced to leave Sion at the royal dragon stable. It wasn't very large, and it wasn't underground like the Citadel's, but it was beautiful. Numerous stone arches connected to pillars sculpted of white marble, forming the entrances to the individual stalls. The pillars were inlaid with gold and silver bands which told me that the king had more money than he knew what to do with.

Sion was wary at first, but I convinced her everything was fine and she disappeared into the stall she'd been given. I followed Maren as she navigated her way through the palace, and the guards stayed with us the entire way. We reached two doors that were taller than what seemed necessary and Maren stopped.

"On the other side of those doors is the throne room," Maren said quietly.

I nodded, not realizing the gravity of her statement. As she stared at me intently, realization slowly dawned on me.

"The king is in there," I said. "Your father."

"Yes."

Maren's usual carefree persona was dampened. She hadn't talked much about her father, so I knew little other than the fact that he was the king. I had noticed that she didn't like being around him, which

I suspected was part of the reason she chose to become a rider.

I tried to keep calm, but my heart started racing and I was getting anxious about meeting the king. Were there certain times I should speak? Should I speak at all? What kind of rules or protocols were there when meeting royalty? All of these questions and more swirled around inside my mind and I could feel Sion put up a wall to shield herself from my thoughts.

"I'll do the talking," Maren said. "Just stand beside me for support."

"Sounds easy enough," I replied.

"We'll see."

While we were talking, one of the guards had slipped inside the throne room. He returned a moment later and servants dressed in nondescript clothing pushed the giant doors open. A noble came walking out of the throne room and paused briefly to offer a bow to Maren.

"Princess," he greeted, then continued on his way.

"That's Lord Rowe. He's one of the only nobles I can stomach."

The leader of the guards glanced at Maren and shook his head, then stepped into the throne room. I decided I didn't like the man. He was too serious.

"What's his name?" I whispered, nodding toward the leader.

"That's Barclay," Maren replied. "He's the captain of my father's riders."

"Your father has his own group of riders?"

"Technically speaking, they're part of the Citadel, but everyone knows they're really his personal riders. Barclay and the others swore oaths of allegiance to my father long before they bonded with their dragons, so their loyalty lies with the crown."

"I'm surprised the Citadel allowed the bonding at all," I said.

"They had little choice in the matter. If they didn't allow it, my father would likely have stormed the place. Master Pevus made the wise choice of allowing it to avoid violence. Unfortunately, my father is no different than other nobles you've encountered."

Perhaps I had romanticized the role of a king in my mind, but I had always assumed the leader of Osnen was moral and just. To hear that he was like every other pompous noble I'd met was disappointing.

Maren entered the throne room and I walked beside her just as she'd asked. The room was filled with signs of wealth. Detailed marble and bronze statues of armored men lined the pathway that led to the throne, and the floor was covered with a plush purple rug that made my boots sink into it as I walked.

Three stairs led up to an ovular dais where the

throne sat. The back of the chair stood at least five feet high and was gilded with gold. It was cushioned all the way up with bright red material. A black curtain, trimmed in gold, outlined the dais. It was pinned in place on either side, giving me a perfect view of the king.

Erling Toft was completely different from what I had envisioned. Maren was beautiful, and I assumed both of her parents would be as well. My assumption couldn't have been further from the truth. Erling was bald and had a gray goatee that thinned past his chin and stretched up the sides of his face, ending evenly near the tops of his ears. In the middle of his forehead, and running down the left side of his face, was a blotchy red-purplish bruise.

"Try not to stare," Maren whispered.

I quickly averted my gaze to the left and pretended to admire the obvious display of opulence. Maren halted a few feet from the stairs and bowed. I followed her example and watched her from the corner of my eye to know when to rise. When she did, I hurried to mirror her.

"Daughter," Erling greeted. His tone was deep and he spoke loudly enough that his voice carried throughout the room and echoed back to us.

"Father," Maren replied.

An awkward silence ensued and I wondered what the cause of their strained relationship was. I felt out of place and clasped my hands behind my back.

"New servant?" Erling asked, turning his gaze on me.

"He's not a servant," Maren said. "He's my … friend. And a fellow rider."

"Your friend, huh? I see." Erling stroked his beard repeatedly. "From what I hear, you aren't a rider anymore. Your dragon was killed, yes?"

Maren didn't flinch or show the slightest crack in her demeanor, but I knew that his remark had struck her the same as a blow would have.

"Yes, my dragon was killed in battle against the dracolich, but that doesn't mean I'm not a rider anymore."

"Sure it does," Erling replied. "You can only bond with one dragon. If that dragon is dead, then you are unable to call yourself a rider."

"What does it matter?" Maren demanded, her anger starting to boil over.

"It matters because you have duties and responsibilities here at court that you've been neglecting while you spent the last few months gallivanting around at the Citadel. Not to mention your mother has been worried sick about you. If it weren't for my spies at the Citadel, I'd have thought you dead."

That last part was a surprise. The king had spies within the Citadel? Then again, so had the Necromancer. They were two sides of the same coin, it seemed.

"What responsibilities? To sit beside you in silence and look pretty? I want more out of life than that."

"You'll have more," Erling said. "I've been in talks with our allies in the west and Prince Marcel has agreed to marry you. So, you see, you'll have plenty of responsibility with strengthening our kingdom outside of Osnen."

My stomach turned and I thought I was going to be sick. Not this again. First, it was Hrodin. Now, it was whoever Prince Marcel was. Perhaps I had fallen in love with the wrong woman. As soon as that thought entered my mind, I berated myself. Maren was everything I wanted and more. Much more. Too much somedays, but that's what made our relationship so agonizingly beautiful.

"I'm not marrying someone for your convenience," Maren replied.

"That's what princes and princesses do. They follow the will of their father, the will of their *king*." Erling emphasized the last word and I realized he wasn't as bad as the nobles I'd dealt with before.

He was worse.

Much worse, Sion's voice chimed into my thoughts.

I hadn't thought it possible, but I found Erling to be more terrible than even Hrodin. Yet, he was right. He was the king, the highest authority in the land. If he ordered something, what could anyone say or do otherwise?

A glance at Maren revealed her face was flushed with anger. I could see the fire in her eyes, that rebellious made-up-her-mind inferno that I had seen many times. Things were about to get ugly. I grabbed Maren's hand and she turned to me, startled out of her anger.

"Breathe," I whispered. "Try to stay calm."

I could feel Erling's eyes on me and I released Maren's hand and turned my attention to her father. I heard Maren take a deep breath.

"I'm not marrying someone I don't even know. That may be what you and mother were forced into, but I refuse to play the political games. Traditions will never change until you stop following them."

Erling laughed. "You talk as if you have a choice," he said. "You don't have a choice. You will do as I say and you'll pretend to be happy doing it."

"Your Majesty," I said.

Maren tried to stop me, but I moved around her and stepped closer to the throne. I hadn't noticed the guards standing behind the curtain, and they stepped out of hiding to reveal themselves. One of them drew his sword and leaped in front of Erling protectively. I held my hands up to show I wasn't a threat.

"Your Majesty," I repeated. "May I speak?"

Erling stared at me for a moment, then waved his guards off. They disappeared back behind the curtain and I blew a sigh of relief.

"What is your name, boy?" Erlin asked.

"Eldwin, sir. Eldwin Baines."

Erling's eye twitched at the name and he rose from his throne.

"Don't let her go anywhere," Erling commanded his guards. "Eldwin and I are going to take a walk."

10

Erling led me out of the throne room and down an enormous hall in the south wing of the palace. He walked a few steps ahead of me and had his hands clasped behind his back. I was eager to hear what he wanted to say, but at the same time, I was nervous. His reaction to my surname was concerning.

At the end of the hall, the palace was open to the outside. A wide, circular balcony offered a magnificent view of the city below. The edge of the platform had stonework railings to keep one from falling off the edge, but it was short enough that you could still climb over it.

"Tell me what you see, Eldwin."

I glanced at the king uncertainly, but he kept his focus ahead. I looked out at the city and considered what sort of answer he was expecting. Was this a trick question? Or perhaps a test?

"I see the future of Osnen," I replied.

Eling's stoic expression broke a little and I caught the glimpse of a smile.

"Very astute," Erling said. "And very vague."

The king turned to face me. I did my best to look him in the eyes instead of staring at his bruised face.

"I have worked hard to make this kingdom what

it is, and yet there are still people in this world who seek to tear it down."

"You mean the False King?" I asked.

"Him too," Erling said. "I'm talking about the common man. Those who feel that this world is somehow unfair. They seek to change the way things are, to destroy what others have done before them. People like you, Eldwin."

I scrunched my face in confusion. "I'm sorry? I don't understand what you mean."

"I'm not a fool, boy. I saw the way you looked at my daughter. You are a *low born*, a fact you would do well to remember. The title your father earned through his deeds doesn't change your birth."

"Did you meet my father?" I asked.

"Only when I gave him his lands. I didn't want to give him anything, not even the title, but the nobles were overwhelming in their support of him. In my opinion, low borns don't deserve anything. Their life is reward enough."

Erling was making me angry. Whether he was a king or not, I didn't agree with him. And I certainly didn't think anyone should hold such beliefs.

"Why did you bring me out here?" I asked.

Erling walked to the edge of the balcony. I was tempted to leave, but I knew that would likely anger him and his guards would be all over me. I joined him and waited for him to speak.

"I don't want you to see or speak to Maren ever again. In exchange, I'll double the holdings I gave your father. I'll also send workers to your lands to get the crops growing again. And you can have the pick of any daughter among my nobles as your wife."

I was stunned. The king was trying to bribe me? I blinked several times, trying to wrap my mind around his words. As I thought about it, I don't know why I was so surprised. Nobles were shady, so why would their leader be any different? The silence stretched long enough that it felt awkward. I cleared my throat.

"I'm sorry, Your Majesty, but I can't do that. I, uh … I'm in love with Maren and I could never hurt her like that."

Erling's demeanor changed so drastically I thought he had two personalities. He turned and grabbed me by the front of my shirt and slammed me into the railing.

I'll burn that man to ash, Sion growled in my mind.

No! I'm fine.

"Do you know that I could have you executed for any reason at all? In fact, I don't even need a reason. I could hurl you off this balcony right now and no one would think twice about your disappearance."

Let him try, Sion said. *He'll have an inferno to deal with.*

His face had turned red with his anger and he looked like he was barely containing his rage. My heart was racing in my chest and I thought for sure he was going to push me off the balcony. I swallowed hard and tried not to look frightened. Sion's fury filled the bond and I was afraid she was going to do something foolish.

Erling leaned closer, his breath hot against my face. "I hold all the power here, Eldwin. So long as you are in Osnen, you are nothing more than the dirt beneath my feet. And I'll trample you if I must."

"Father!"

I looked past the king to see Maren. Guards came rushing behind her and despite the situation, I smiled. It seemed no one could stop her from doing whatever she wanted. Erling released me and turned around to face her.

"Leave Eldwin alone!" Maren demanded.

Erling held up a hand and his guards halted their advance.

"You are royalty and I will not have our family name tarnished because you want to gallivant around with a low born!"

"Stop it!" Maren screamed. "Stop trying to control everyone! I'm so sick of this, of you! I don't know how my mother has put up with you all this time. I would have run away or stabbed you in your sleep."

Maren's outburst surprised Erling as much as it surprised me. He became like a statue, unmoving and silent. I walked away from the railing and stood beside Maren. She grabbed my mangled hand and glared defiantly at her father.

"You don't get a choice," Erling finally said. His eyes went from Maren to me for a brief moment, then back to Maren. His tone didn't sound as dangerous now, but his fists were clenched.

"If this is what you think our family name represents, this hateful attitude towards anyone you think is less than you, then I want no part of it," Maren said.

The two stared at one another in a silent battle of wills. Maren was the most stubborn and rebellious person I had ever met, but her father was a close second. He was also entitled, which made him dangerous.

"I want him out of my sight, now. And as for you, daughter, maybe a few days in solitude away from this low born will get your mind straight."

Maren snapped her fiery gaze at the guards as they started to come toward me. They hesitated, glancing at Erling for guidance.

"If they lay a hand on him, you'll regret it," Maren threatened her father.

Erling smirked. "You're cute when you're angry. You almost remind me of myself."

"Eldwin and I are leaving."

"I'll say when you can leave," Erling replied.

Maren looked at me, her eyes meeting mine.

She stared so intently it was like she was peering into my soul. She smiled and nodded, but I wasn't sure what she was thinking. Whatever it was, she had made up her mind about it. She turned back to her father.

"I claim the Right of Secession," Maren said.

Erling's face betrayed his stoicism for a split second, but then his face hardened again. He crossed his arms over his chest.

"If you do this, there's no turning back. You'll be dead to me *and* your mother."

"I'm aware of the consequences."

"Are you sure? This is your last chance," Erling said.

"I've never been more sure of anything," Maren replied. "I hereby claim the Right of Secession. I choose love, father. Love over privilege."

Erling's left eye twitched and he turned his back to us. I wasn't sure what was happening. What was the Right of Secession? I looked at Maren questioningly, but she shook her head slightly.

"Your claim is acknowledged," Erling said without turning around. "Leave now and never return."

Maren spun on her heels and pulled me along. We headed out of the palace and stopped at the royal stable. Sion was pacing in her stall, her powerful tail flicking back and forth with her agitation.

Let's get out of here, I told her as I opened the door to the stall.

I'd like to chomp on his bones, she replied. *How dare he touch you!*

It's fine, I said, trying to calm her. *Nothing happened and he didn't hurt me.*

Sion didn't reply, but I could feel through the bond she was still simmering with rage. We followed Maren around to the south side of the stable to a rectangular platform that was designed for dragons to take flight. Maren climbed up Sion's shoulder and got into the saddle. I glanced back, half expecting to see guards coming for us, but there was no one. I scrambled up Sion's scales and into the saddle in front of Maren.

Head east, I told Sion. *We're continuing the same way we were going before we were stopped.*

Sion launched herself into the air, her outstretched wings catching the wind and forcing us upward. She flapped her wings and added to our momentum, ascending higher and higher until we were far above the city.

"What happened?" I asked, shouting over the wind. "What's the Right of Secession?"

"I forsook my royalty. I'm as good as a low born now."

11

Once we left the city behind, Maren revealed she had lost her focus on the trail of magic we'd been following during the argument with her father. It took some time, but she eventually tracked it down again and we were heading to the next location.

Since Maren was focused on her spell, she remained silent. That left me with a lot of time to think, and I couldn't get her words out of my head. She'd forsaken her royalty. For me. It was hard to fathom that. I'd do anything for Maren, but given my social status in life, that limited me. She had literally given up everything for me. It made me feel loved in such a different and profound way.

You humans are so odd, Sion said, chuckling.

How do you mean?

You think about love as if there are different forms of it. It's interesting.

Do dragons feel love? I asked.

We do, but there is only one form of love. We love all things equally.

That sounds a lot simpler, I said.

It is less dramatic, Sion confirmed.

I laughed and rubbed the scales along Sion's neck. She hummed in response and I felt Maren tap my shoulder. I glanced back at her. Her eyes were closed, but she was pointing ahead. I looked in the direction of where she was pointing, but other than a vast forest, I didn't see anything.

Maren's pointing at something. Do you see anything? I asked Sion.

I can feel magic. And wards. Whatever it is, someone doesn't want visitors.

Great. Find a place to land. I have a feeling we're going to have to walk the rest of the way.

My stomach lurched as Sion descended and Maren wrapped her arms around my chest. We landed in a small clearing amidst the trees. It was barely wide enough for Sion's wingspan, but she managed to land without hurting herself. Maren and I dismounted and I grabbed our packs from the saddle.

Do you want to come with us? I asked Sion.

Yes.

I pulled the collar off the saddle and put it around Sion's neck. Her shape and size shrunk and shifted until she was in her human form. Maren pulled some clothes from her pack and handed them to Sion. While we waited for her to get dressed, I looked around the woods. Birds sang in the treetops and I could hear animals moving through the brush. The place didn't look ominous at all, but it felt that way.

"Sion said there are wards in here. Will they prevent us from getting to where the magic is flowing?"

Maren shook her head. "They shouldn't. I can sense the wards, but they aren't defensive magic. I'm not sure what they're warding against, but they are active. I guess we'll find out as we get closer."

She didn't sound too concerned, so I tried not to let it bother me.

I'm ready, Sion said.

"Lead the way," I told Maren. She walked ahead of me and we began weaving our way through the trees. I spotted a few game trails, but otherwise, there were no defined paths.

"I get the feeling no one has been here in a while," I said.

"You're probably right," Maren replied. "If dragons don't even know about the Assembly, how would anyone else?"

"Good point."

"Those are the only kind I make," Maren said with a laugh.

I rolled my eyes at her, but I also smiled. It was good to see her not being so serious and stressed. I wanted to talk about what she'd done by giving up her royalty, but I didn't feel like it was the right time yet. I decided that once we stopped Demris, however that happened, then I would broach the subject.

It was difficult to tell how long we'd been walking, but I was suddenly tired. My lungs felt constricted like I wasn't getting enough air, and my muscles weakened as a result. Maren seemed to be struggling as well, but not as much as I was. A glance back at Sion revealed she didn't seem fazed at all.

"Any idea how much further it is?" I huffed.

"The magic is tethered just up here," Maren replied. "We're very close."

The trees thinned as we continued and then we found ourselves in a glade. It was a large open space ringed in a complete circle by trees. The grassy meadow was beautiful, but I didn't spot a foundation as we had at the other locations.

"There's nothing here?" I said quizzically. "Do you still sense the magic?"

Maren nodded slowly, but she had a confused look on her face. "That's so strange," she muttered.

"What is?"

"I could have sworn the magic was tethered here, but as soon as we stepped into the clearing, it was gone. Now I feel it over there." Maren pointed to the left.

"Maybe you made a mistake? Or maybe the magic moved?"

"Maybe," Maren replied. "I don't know."

We headed in the direction she pointed and the exhaustion I felt strengthened. We reached another clearing, but it looked eerily similar to the one we'd just left. I started to suspect that the wards were intended to confuse people and turn them around so that they gave up looking for whatever was out here.

"Maybe we should start over from where we landed," I suggested.

"No, then we'd be backtracking. This has to be the way because I can still feel the magic."

Do you feel the magic, too? I asked Sion.

Yes, but it's slippery. Every time I think I've latched onto it, it slips away.

"What is happening?" I asked aloud, but neither Sion nor Maren replied. We just kept walking, following Maren's direction. And every time we reached another glade where the magic was tethered, it turned out to be the wrong place again.

I was getting frustrated, but my exhaustion was becoming overwhelming. I began to see things that weren't there. From my peripheral, I could see shadows among the trees whispering and pointing at us, but when I looked at them directly, they were gone. It could have been my imagination, but it felt so real.

My legs gave out on me and I collapsed to the ground. Maren turned to look at me and through blurred vision, I could see that her face was red and she was trying to stay steady on her feet.

"I'm fine," I said. "I just need a minute."

I looked at Sion. She had curled up into a ball on the ground behind me.

I'm tired, she said.

She looked so comfortable that it made me lie down. I stared up at the canopy and it started to spin, so I closed my eyes and that was all I remembered.

When I awoke, I had no idea where I was. I thought we had been in a forest, but my memory was hazy. I blinked several times and sat up. Maren was passed out a few feet in front of me and Sion was standing nearby.

This is a strange place, she said. *When we fell asleep, we were out there,* Sion motioned behind us. *Yet now we are here. The wards are behind us, but the flow of magic is tethered to that building.*

I looked ahead and saw a temple. It was tall and built of black stones that glinted under the sunlight. I realized we were in another clearing, this one much larger than the others we'd found. I crawled over to Maren and pushed some loose strands of hair behind her ear. Her eyelids fluttered open and she smiled.

"We found it," I said. "Or rather, it found us."

I helped Maren to her feet and she looked at the temple. Her confusion was obvious and she looked at me questioningly. I shrugged.

"I'm not sure how it happened, but we're on the other side of the wards. Sion says this temple is where the magic leads."

"Yes, it does." Maren rubbed her eyes and straightened her hair with her fingers.

"There doesn't appear to be any guards or anything," I said. "I think it should be safe to go inside."

There are dragons inside, Sion said. I could feel her excitement through the bond. *One is coming now.*

I looked at the entrance of the temple and spotted movement. It was the elderly woman, Tyrval the Cold. She hobbled down the stone steps that led to where we were, a smile plastered across her face.

"You found us," she said, a hint of pride in her voice.

"Yes, but it was almost impossible," I replied. "The only reason we found any sort of clue was by complete accident."

"Sometimes fate uses accidents to orchestrate its events."

"You said if we found you that you could help us with Demris. Innocent people are dying while we've been on this quest."

"Whose fault is that?" Tyrval asked.

"Where the blame rests doesn't matter," Maren said. "What matters is stopping him."

Tyrval extended her hand toward the temple. "Step inside. Perhaps the fact that you found our fortress will help convince the others to aid you."

12

The interior of the temple mirrored the exterior in that it was composed of black stone. There were no tapestries on the walls and no rugs lining the floor. The atmosphere felt like a cave. It was dim, slightly humid, and held the scent of aged parchment.

Tyrval walked ahead of us, her pace slow but steady. She moved with a slight hunch as if she had born the weight of something heavy for a long time. I figured that was attributed to her age. It made me curious, too, if staying in human form using the collar had anything to do with it.

"How long have you been here?" Maren asked, breaking my line of thought.

"Me, or the Assembly?"

"Both."

"I've called this place my home for three centuries, but the Assembly has been here since the beginning of human and dragon bonding."

"Three *centuries?*" Maren asked incredulously. "I didn't think dragons lived that long."

"Bonded dragons don't," Tyrval confirmed. "Myself and the other members of the Assembly have never been bonded to a human. If a human bonds with a young dragon and dies at a ripe old age, the dragon may live for another fifty years."

"Why do bonded dragons have shorter life spans?" I asked.

"I'm not sure, but I think it has to do with the link that forms between the two. Dragons in the wild don't form emotional connections except with their mates. Humans are very emotional creatures, and I think that strains dragons in some way. I could be completely off the mark, of course, so take that with some skepticism."

I could see the logic in her theory, but I also believed that humans brought more value to the bond than they did a detriment. Since Tyrval had never bonded with a human, she probably couldn't understand the relationship as fully as a dragon that had.

Yes, I think you are right, Sion said. *I do not feel that our bond is a negative thing.*

Sion's words bolstered my opinion even more.

"Where are the others?" Maren asked. "Do they know we're here?"

"Not quite," Tyrval replied. I couldn't see her face, but I knew she was probably grinning.

"What does that mean? You told Eldwin to find you, so they should have been expecting us, right?"

"No. What I told Eldwin was between the two of us. I did not consult the others before communicating with him."

That gave me pause. If the others, especially Nemryth, didn't know I was coming, this could get ugly.

Don't worry about this Nemryth, Sion said. *I will not let any harm come to you.*

She's the one who broke our bond on the island, I replied. *I don't think she's one to trifle with.*

Sion snorted in response, but I could feel a hint of uncertainty from her in the bond.

We entered a door to the right and I immediately recognized the room as the one I'd been in while being tested on the island. The long table was there, and all the members of the Assembly save for Tyrval were seated at it. Their voices died as soon as they saw us coming.

Nemryth rose from her seat so quickly, the chair skittered back and almost tipped over. She clearly hadn't changed.

"What are *you* doing here?" Her tone held the promise of death, just like her eyes.

Sion stepped around me and stood protectively in front of me, a low growl in her throat. Tyrval ignored all of them and approached the table.

"They have found our fortress and seek our aid," Tyrval said. She took her seat at the table.

"I don't care what they're here for. I should rip your bond away and drop you into the sea!"

"Calm yourself, Nemryth," Tyrval rebuked. "Whatever your feelings towards the boy, we must admit we made a mistake with our judgment."

"The Assembly doesn't make mistakes,"

Nemryth snapped.

"Then explain why the Path restored the bond we revoked."

Nemryth's angry bluster became subdued and an awkward silence stretched between the two dragons. I wondered again why they took the form of humans, but I suspected I would not get an answer to that.

There was a man whose collar had emeralds in it and he leaned forward and whispered something to the others I couldn't make out. I had the vague memory that his name was Brold, but the entire ordeal felt like a bad dream and the details were fuzzy. The name was the only thing that had stuck.

Tyrval motioned for us to come closer. I patted Sion's shoulder and closed the distance to the table. Maren stood beside me and clasped my hand in hers.

"What is your request?" Nemryth asked. It was clear by her expression that she was struggling to be civil.

I knew before I spoke that this would not be an easy task, but the Assembly was our only hope at stopping Demris. I cleared my throat.

"When we returned from the Island of Lost Souls, we brought back the soul of Maren's dragon. Something happened once we made it back, but I'm not sure what. He killed the helmsman of the ferry and he's been killing more people since then. We've tried to stop him, but the task seems impossible."

"What do you want from us?" Vandir asked. He was the dragon that seemed more like a human noble than anything else. "What do the affairs of men have to do with us?"

"Nothing, I guess. You've locked yourselves away from the world for so long that not even dragons remember you. I feared coming here was a mistake." I wasn't really upset. I'd met them all before and knew that there would be pushback, so I had decided to bluff. Maren looked at me, the confusion evident on her face.

I winked at her as I turned away from the table and started for the door. When we were only a few steps from exiting the room, I began to worry that Nemryth wouldn't take the bait.

"Halt," she called out.

A wave of relief washed over me and I turned around.

"You doubt the power of this council? Did our previous judgment of you not display what we are capable of?"

"I can't say that it did," I replied.

Nemryth glared at me. "You test my patience. You bring a soul back from death and cause a disaster and think to place that problem at *my* feet? I will not tolerate such disrespect."

"I apologize," I said. "I can see how it sounds that way to you, but that was not my intent. I only wish to stop the death of innocent people."

"What were you trying to accomplish?" Brold asked.

"Demris was Maren's dragon. He died in the battle against the False King."

"We are aware," Nemryth said.

"Maren was crushed. When she found him on the island, I couldn't bear seeing her in anguish anymore. I told her to bring him back. If someone is to be blamed, it is me and me alone. Regardless of that blame, I humbly ask for the Assembly's help. We only wanted to bring Demris's soul back to his body so that he could be with Maren again."

"Where is his body?" Vandir asked.

"At the Citadel," Maren answered. "I cast a preservation spell on him so that he wouldn't decompose."

Nemryth looked at each member of the Assembly, one by one. It became apparent they were holding some sort of telepathic conversation. Maren squeezed my hand and I returned the gesture.

Nemryth radiates power and authority, Sion said. *You were right to warn me earlier. She is a foe that I do not think I could defeat.*

I think she is the head of the Assembly. If she isn't, she should be.

"The Assembly will help you," Nemryth announced. Vandir stood and left the room. I assumed he had been outvoted and didn't want to be part of helping us.

"Demris is not a rogue soul killing at random. He is seeking a body to hold him, any kind of body. Unfortunately for those unlucky enough to encounter him, they aren't strong enough to hold the soul of a dragon. The result is death."

"I told you," Maren whispered at me.

"There is something that can hold his soul besides his own body," Nemryth continued. Vandir returned carrying a small box and he set it on the table in front of Nemryth. She opened the box and removed something from within it.

"This is a soul stone. They were created long ago to imprison errant dragons, those who refused to submit to the Assembly's decision of allowing our hatchlings to bond with humans."

"We don't want to imprison Demris," I said.

"Yes, I know. The stone will hold his soul until you can release him into his own body. I will show you how to use it."

"Thank you so much!" Maren exclaimed. "I am indebted to you."

"No," Nemryth said. "Eldwin is indebted to us. He is to blame for this problem, and he will bear the responsibility. And I have a request."

"Anything," I said, blurting out the words before fully thinking about what Nemryth would ask of me.

"Once you have dealt with Demris, you are to

bring this stone back to us."

"I will. How will I find this place again?" I asked.

Nemryth laughed. "You don't find the Temple of the Bond," she said. "It finds you."

13

We left the Temple of the Bond behind, armed with the soul stone and ready to confront Demris one final time. As we neared the capital, I told Sion to keep a wide berth to avoid any trouble. A strong wind picked up that blew in our favor and we made the trip back to the Terranese border quicker than I expected.

The only obstacle now was to figure out where Demris was. Since he'd stayed within the general vicinity of the Terranese school so far, I hoped he was still there. Sion landed near a small town once we crossed the border and Maren and I went into the local inn for some food. I was also hoping we might hear some news that would direct us to Demris. A handful of people were inside, and they weren't very talkative.

"This place seems slower than when we came through a few days ago," I said.

"A lot slower," Maren agreed.

A skinny barmaid approached our table and greeted us with a tired smile. She was missing one of her front teeth and smelled like she hadn't bathed in weeks. I did my best not to breathe through my nose.

"What'll you have?" She asked.

"Do you have any soup?"

"Potato soup. Or you can have just broth."

"I'll take the potatoes," I said.

"Good choice. I like potato soup, too." Her smile intensified before she looked at Maren. "What about you?"

"I'll have the same thing," Maren replied.

The barmaid left and Maren grinned at me.

"What?" I asked.

"She likes you," Maren giggled.

I shook my head. "No, she doesn't."

"She certainly does! Not that I blame her. You're a good man, Eldwin. People can sense that about you."

I wanted to wait until after we'd dealt with Demris, but I couldn't contain my curiosity any longer. "Why did you forsake your royalty?" I asked. "And what exactly does that mean?"

The barmaid returned with two bowls and set them on the table. Steam rose from the soup and it smelled delicious.

"Do you want some ale to wash it down with?"

"Thank you, no," I replied. "Some water would be great, though."

"I would love some water, too," Maren said.

The barmaid nodded and went to the bar, then returned a moment later with two wooden mugs of water. I pulled a few coins from my purse and handed them to the barmaid. She smiled and went to check on the other patrons and I turned my attention back to Maren. She was eating her soup and kept her eyes on the table.

"Well?" I asked.

"Well what?"

I stared at her until she looked up at me. I raised my eyebrows expectantly.

"I gave up my title because I don't want to be part of my father's legacy," Maren said. "He thinks that he can bully anyone into doing what he wants because he's the king. And I don't want to be forced into some political marriage. I want …"

"What? What do you want?" I asked.

"I want to be with you, Eldwin. I love you."

Those words were like a beautiful majestic song to my ears. Any doubts I had about my feelings toward her disappeared.

"I love you, too," I said, and I meant it.

"I'm no longer a princess. All the benefits of my title are gone. I have no money, no birthright, and no home. I have nothing."

"You have me," I said.

"And that's all I need."

I had no idea how we would make it in the world, but since we were going to return to study at the Citadel, we had some time to figure things out. I still couldn't believe she'd given up everything, but

I was determined to do whatever was needed to take care of her.

You have a good heart for a human, Sion said.

Most humans have good hearts, I replied.

Not the ones I've known.

You have a valid point considering the people in your history, but I think you'll change your mind as you meet more of us.

Maren and I finished our food and left the inn. There had been very little conversation among the other patrons, and none of it regarded Demris.

"Let's get closer to the school," I suggested. "I'm sure he's still in the same area."

"I hope so," Maren said.

We flew west until the sun was about to set. Sion landed in an open field and we spent the night on the uncomfortable ground. When morning came, neither of us had slept much. Maren continuously dozed off in the saddle. I could tell when she did because her weight shifted and I had to lean forward to keep from waking her.

My eyes were heavy and threatening to close on me when Sion's voice shattered my drowsiness.

Look! I think I see Demris!

I shook myself awake and scanned the ground below. There was a floating cloud of green smoke heading toward a town. People were running in the opposite direction, but we were too high to hear their cries of panic and fear.

Get us down there, I sold Sion. *Hurry!*

She dived down without warning. Maren cried out in surprise and grabbed onto me. The wind whipped violently around us, and I had to close my eyes because it felt like I was going to be permanently blinded. I felt Sion level out and my breakfast threatened to make a reappearance.

He's possessed someone! Sion shouted. *Go!*

I leaped from the saddle before Sion could land and hit to the ground, using my momentum to roll forward so I didn't hurt myself. I staggered to my feet and a wave of dizziness hit me. Sion landed ahead and Maren dismounted.

"The gemstone!" Maren cried out. "I need the gemstone!"

In my adrenaline-fueled leap, I'd forgotten that it was in my pack—which was still attached to Sion's saddle. I pointed at Sion.

"It's in my bag!"

Maren retrieved the gemstone and rushed into the town. My dizziness faded and I hurried to catch up with her. A woman screamed and we spotted a man clawing at his own throat. I guessed the woman was his wife and I ran to her, pulling her away from the horrific sight.

The man was gasping, his face bright red. Thick veins protruded along his neck and I had the feeling his head might explode. Maren reached the man and quickly cast a spell that forced Demris from the man's body. Green smoke funneled out of the man's mouth and the redness began to diminish.

Once the entirety of Demris's soul was free, Maren held the gemstone up and spoke the words needed to activate the magic. The black gemstone flashed once, twice, three times, then it began to suck the smoke into itself. An unearthly cry filled the air, a haunting sound that pulled at my heart.

The man coughed and wheezed but was otherwise uninjured. I released the woman and she rushed to embrace him. Maren looked at me and nodded. She clutched the gemstone close to her body and we headed back to meet Sion.

"Are you all right?" I asked.

"I'm fine," Maren replied. "I'm glad we got here when we did. If we'd been a few minutes later …"

"But we weren't," I said. "And that man and his family are shaken up, but he's alive. I'll take that victory any day."

"Me too."

We climbed into the saddle and I rubbed Sion's neck, thankful that she had spotted Demris while Maren and I were dozing off.

Thank you, I told her. *You just saved that man's life.*

Maren saved him. I just helped a little.

I smiled and leaned back against Maren. She wrapped her arms around me and kissed the back of my neck. We had finally stopped Demris's unintentional reign of terror and things felt a little more normal now.

"Let's go home," I said, the words meant for both of my companions.

14

Returning to the Citadel was a welcome reprieve from the last few weeks. The sight of it in the distance set me at ease, and once we landed in the courtyard, I truly felt like I had come home after years of being away.

Maren took the gemstone and headed straight for the underground stable. A few riders glanced at her curiously but didn't stop her. I climbed down from Sion's back and stretched my legs, then hurried after her.

The cave that served as the stable was dark and cool, with only a few torches along the walls. I knew that a larger dragon had carried Demris's body back to the Citadel after the battle against the False King, but I didn't know where exactly they had placed him.

"Maren?" I called out.

"Here," she answered. A ball of glowing light erupted into life and I saw she was at the very end of the cavern. As I passed under the hidden door in the ceiling, it reminded me of when Maren and I had first met. I laughed when I thought about how we ended up in the women's bathing chamber and how embarrassed I was. That day felt like it had happened so long ago.

Maren and I had gone through so much and yet we'd barely stepped onto the path that was life. It was hard to believe. I stood a few feet away from Maren and stared at Demris's body. The preservation spell had kept his body in pristine condition. If I hadn't known any better, I would have assumed that Demris was merely sleeping. The only indication that something wasn't right was the faint glow his body gave off.

"I hope this works," Maren whispered.

"It will," I said, but I had my doubts. The Assembly, specifically Nemryth, scared me. They thought themselves better than humans, and the sentiment reminded me of nobles and their view of low borns. I assumed the only reason they helped us was because ultimately, they were helping one of their own.

Maren knelt in front of Demris's body and lifted the left side of his mouth open, then placed the gemstone inside. She rose and stepped back, then closed her eyes and muttered the words Nemryth had instructed.

A tremor shook the ground and dust filtered down from the ceiling. There was a loud hissing sound and then Demris's body started convulsing. His legs twitched sporadically, and his chest began to move as if he was breathing. Maren whispered more words and the glow coming off Demris slowly faded.

"The preservation spell is gone," she said, glancing at me. I could see the uncertainty in her face, but I smiled and tried to appear confident. Maren turned back to Demris just as his eyes flared open. He opened his mouth and wheezed in a deep breath, causing the gemstone to slip off his tongue and clatter onto the ground. Maren retrieved it and handed it to me. I tried to put it into my coin purse, but it was too large to fit so I just held onto it.

Maren suddenly gasped and my heart fell into my stomach, but when she turned to look at me, she was smiling. Tears rolled down from her eyes.

"I can feel him," she said, choking over the words. "I can feel the bond again!"

Relief washed over me. Her gasp made me think the worst had happened. Maren rushed forward and embraced Demris's face with her arms, sobbing with joy.

Did it work? Sion asked.

Yes, I replied. *It worked. He's alive and well.*

Sion flooded the bond with excitement and I burst into laughter. Everything felt right in the world. There were no more enemies to fight, no more obstacles to undergo, no more heartache to endure. It was just the four of us and we were home.

There is one last task, Sion said.

What?

We must return the gemstone.

In the joy of the moment, I'd almost forgotten about it. I held it up and inspected it in the light of Maren's magical globe. Its multifaceted surface reflected the light despite its dark color. I didn't want to leave, but I knew that I had to keep my word to the Assembly. I would go, but it could wait one more day.

Sion came into the stable and curled up in one of the alcoves. Her eyes watched me until she slowly drifted off to sleep. I wanted to sleep, too, but we had a long story to share with Master Anesko. Maren didn't want to leave Demris, but he needed to readjust to being in his body and he also fell asleep.

Maren and I left the stable and entered the Citadel. The school had taken on the next group of students and the halls were filled with people I didn't recognize. We eventually found Anesko and related everything we'd experienced, from the Island of Lost Souls to our new knowledge of the Assembly. Anesko listened intently, stopping us a few times to ask questions.

Once our tale had been relayed, we went to the dining hall and ate dinner, then retired to Maren's room. Anesko said the dormitories were completely booked, so I'd have to room with Maren. That didn't bother either one of us. We slept in separate beds and when the morning came, I gave Maren the music box I had bought from the Tajir in the desert when I was with Rory's caravan.

"I love it," Maren said. She twisted the dial and listened to the song, then set it on her side table. We sat in silence for a long while, just enjoying each other's presence. I finally broke the moment and embraced Maren.

"I don't want you to go," she whispered.

"I don't want to go, but I must. Sion and I will be back as quickly as possible."

Maren sighed and released me. "Go on, then. Get out of here so you can hurry up and get back."

I smiled and planted a kiss on her cheek, then went down to the dining hall to grab some breakfast. I ate on the run and within half an hour, Sion and I were in the sky, traveling east to the temple. Having made the journey before and knowing what to expect, it didn't seem to take as long to get to the forest.

Just as before, Sion and I both grew exhausted as we searched for the location of the temple. We settled down to rest and when we woke up, we were in front of it. Nemryth and Tyrval were standing at the top of the steps, waiting.

"I have to admit, I am surprised," Nemryth said.

"About what?" I asked.

"You came back to return the gemstone. I didn't think you would."

"I gave my oath," I said.

"Yes, but until now, the word of a human was worthless to me." She hesitated, then said, "Thank you."

"Is that a hint of gratefulness I'm sensing?" I asked, chuckling.

"Bah! Humans," Nemryth growled. She took the gemstone and stormed into the temple.

Tyrval shook her head, but there was a smile on

her lips.

"Thank you," I told her. "Without you, Demris would still be killing people right now."

"We must work together, no matter the divide that separates us."

I nodded in agreement. "When we were searching for a way to find this place, we came across a monastery of an old cult. They were dragon slayers and their writings mentioned their quest to kill the Assembly. Were you around for that?"

Tyrval's face grew solemn. "Yes, I was there. Those monks came close to achieving their goals, but Nemryth devised a plan to fake our deaths. We used these collars to disguise ourselves as humans and imbued the temple with a multitude of spells."

"Why don't you leave the temple now? You should go and see what the world is like. Those monks died and their order is gone, so I'm certain you have anything to worry about."

"The only certainty in this life is death," Tyrval replied. "The world is much different now than when I was young. This temple is all I have known for most of my existence. I see no reason to venture out now."

I shrugged, agreeing to disagree. "When Nemryth said I was indebted to the Assembly, what did she mean?"

The mischievous look reappeared on Tyrval's face. "If we have need of you, we will call upon you," she said cryptically.

"Right. Well, I'll be off then." I turned to leave but Tyrval stopped me.

"There is something wrong in the world."

"What is it?" I asked.

"I don't know, but I can feel it in my bones."

"The greatest enemy in my lifetime has been defeated, twice," I said. "I think the world is fine."

Tyrval had been locked away in that temple too long, I decided. For once, the world was finally … right. I waved goodbye and Sion and I left the temple. As we flew back to the Citadel, I considered the future. I didn't know what it held, but as long as I had Sion and Maren, I knew life would never be dull.

THE END

ABOUT THE AUTHOR

Richard Fierce is a fantasy and space opera author. He's been writing since childhood, but began publishing in 2007. Since then, he's written multiple novels and short stories.

In 2000, Richard won Poet of the Year for his poem *The Darkness*. He's also one of the creative brains behind the Allatoona Book Festival, a literary event in Acworth, Georgia.

A recovering retail worker, he now works in the tech industry when he's not busy writing.

He's married and has three step-daughters (pray for him), three dogs (two huskies!), three cats, two ferrets and a fish. He basically has a zoo.

His love affair with fantasy was born in high school when a friend's mother gave him a copy of *Dragons of Spring Dawning* by Margaret Weis and Tracy Hickman.

www.ingramcontent.com/pod-product-compliance
Lightning Source LLC
Chambersburg PA
CBHW032039180726
48284CB00008B/2653